Come and ride with us!

Illustrated by Annie Kubler and Caroline Formby

Published by Child's Play (International) Ltd
Swindon   Auburn ME   Sydney
© 1995 Child's Play®   ISBN 0-85953-794-3   Printed in China
Millennium edition 1999   Library of Congress Number 96-47797
A catalogue reference for this book is available from the British Library

HAITI
The buses to the city are always full of people going to market. They are brightly painted and the drivers keep tooting the horn. You can't miss them!

Hello. I'm Sonia.

I'm Sonia. Hurry up, Mother,
or we'll miss the bus.
Children aren't allowed on top.
I hope there's room inside.

CANADA
In the cold far north, it's a special day when the plane brings supplies.

BANGLADESH Rickshaws are everywhere. Some have pretty covers. Pedalling is hard work.

**My name is Abdul. Hey, look at me!
I am riding in a rickshaw with my mother.
If you come with us, we'll take an auto rickshaw.**

Hello. I'm Abdul.

HONG KONG
This busy underground station is on the line from Kowloon to Hong Kong Island. To get there, the train runs in a tunnel under the water.

I am Lee. My grandmother and I are taking a mynah bird to my uncle. I would like to drive a train. Wouldn't you?

PERU   On Lake Titicaca, people live on islands.
Dry reeds are used to build boats and homes.

I am Elsi. Our uncle is taking us fishing.
Can you see the nets and baskets?
"Catch lots of fish," my aunt calls.
Would you like to come and bring us luck?

Hello. I'm Elsi.

I'm Nel. My brother Bart and I are in our new car.
Can you guess where we are going?
We'll make room for you, if you want to come.

BELGIUM AND THE NETHERLANDS
It's flat here, so cycling is easy.
But most people travel by car.

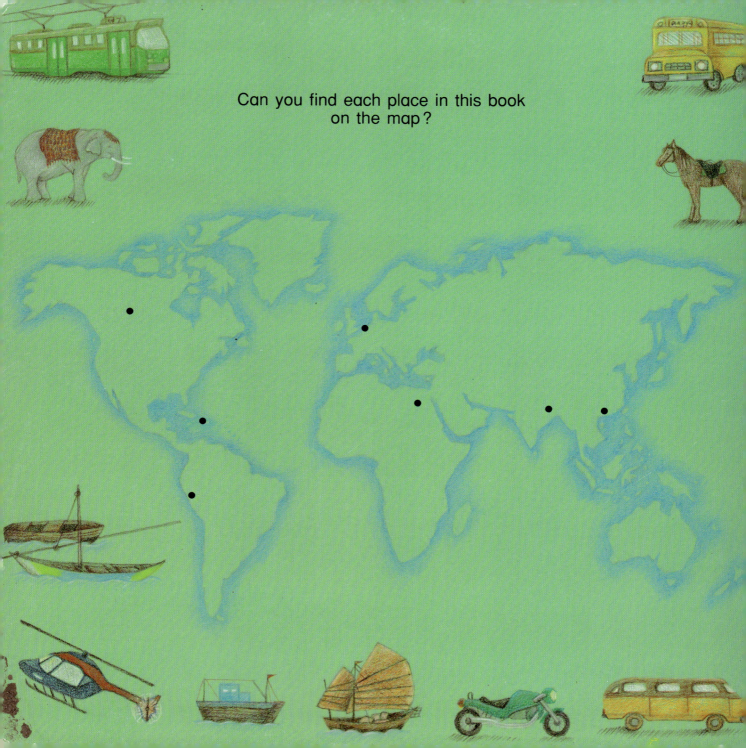